INSIGHT PUBLICA®

Nadakkave, Kozhikode, Kerala, India
+91 4954020666 | +91 9400737475
www.insightpublica.com
e-mail: insightpublica@gmail.com

Melodies
Anjali.A. Nair
(English Poems)
First Edition: March 2021
Copyright©Reserved

ISBN 978-93-90535-93-4

Melodies
Poems

Anjali.A. Nair

DEDICATED TO

THE LOTUS FEET OF BHAGAWAN

SRI SATHYA SAI BABA

Anjali.A. Nair studied in St.Joseph's Anglo - Indian School, Calicut. She took her Bachelors and Masters in English Lit. From Providence Womens College, Calicut and Calicut University respectively, getting a high first class at both levels. Later she took her BEd in English from Calicut Training College. She is fond of writing, specially verses. Her devotion to Sri Sathya Sai Baba is complete.

She has published 5 books; Fervour (Devotional Poems), All is With You - Her experience with Sri. Sathya Sai Baba, *Of Forests, Hills And Dales* is to be released. Distant Lands is to be released including the present.

She is staying with her parents at Saileela, Sadanam Road, Calicut, Mob : 9447174385

ANJALI.A.NAIR

ACKNOWLEDGEMENT

I feel deeply grateful to just about everyone because we were together in fighting the pandemic Corona which propelled the whole world into a web of strong, unified resistance and feelings of love and warm support for each other. God, who is ever cheerful helped me as ever. I am indebted to my parents, Mr Achuthan Nair and Mrs Bharathi. A. Nair, my brother Dinesh. A. Nair, his wife, Meera and son Achuthan for their well wishes. I thank Smt Rekha Sati Raveendran, who got the book ready for publication, and Insight Publica for Publishing it. I must thank you all, too, who would read this book.

Pranam

PREFACE

A Lockdown Paradoxy

I dreamed of being in a passage. When I woke up I felt l was stranded. There appeared very many flights of stairs for me to ascend. I was in a dilemma, harassed and non-plussed. I did not know what to do!. Here where I am, my place, l am fed sumptuously and very cared for. Call it a spiritual quest or longing l need a broad margin where I can lean my piteous self. Alas! there goes the earth under my feet. The mother is good to me when I have normal feelings. People bless, l am happy. My happiness is of a rare nature. It's of an other worldly nature. I don't think it has much to do with the body. Ha! I think, I am bullied much due to this. Enormous strength is required in shouldering hurdles. In life's journey these are unavoidable. Therefore I surrender un-conditionally at the Lotus Feet. My poems are my obligations. Also the happiness I wish to share. These too I place at His Lotus Feet. There is indescribable joy in being eternal. I wish my two eyes would come back to me. They would never gaze at evil. They were always pondering on the Divine Form. Peace fills my heart as l write this. I wish to communicate some joy to you as well.

Poems

NEVER TO TAUNT

I thought I would have to go nowhere!?....
now I am settled in my own vista of hope,
vilification comes as a calling bell outdoor,
make- do - because God chases
the monster outside and home
is surprisingly important, heaven
we are to live intact, inside,
let us pray more, more and more,
happiness and joy are not elusive.

DESOLATE

Granules of sand stretching for miles
make me dizzy, desolate and worn
lone and lorn I'm made out a shrew infuriated!
rugged by boredom, incorrectness and incompleteness
livid with wantonness....
to be casual, careless and whole and
breathe easy,
bold,
I need to roam again
the world.

●

BABA, - AVATAR OF THE AGE

He came from the boundless depths
across many skies
like a orange ball of light gliding,
gliding and....
manifest Himself in the Dravidian land
to enchant, charm, enthrall
His smile belonged to
the goddess of Fortune
He trod gently,
His feet tramping the earth, blessing....,
wherever He went,
He made His mark
leaving the message of love
of amity and kinship
He touched the hearts
of all belonging to the sphere,
with his rhythm and music he captured,!
He was the repository of knowledge,
His words a treatise
His divine Feet are the sole refuge
His role enacted, He is gone!
embossed in the vastness,

the Absolute that fetched Him
ensuring, providing, comforting,
there was not one dry eye at His Samadhi
every man and woman have
a right to call upon Him for
He is as He declared, God,
the Supreme God-head.
●

WHEN JOY WELLS

When joy wells more and more
that joy ineffable which lasts
which extinguishes the jeopardy and peril
it doth tranquil and metamorphosise,
when joy wells,
it is satiating ecstasy,
rhapsody..
bear awhile!
when joy wells so much
resembles bottled soda
that is uncorked.

●

WHERE THE SUN SHINES

The sun hues the earth
scrubbing away its moistness
its scorching rays pierce
the dampness of memories to yield
making change inevitable and
time to lunge in forward direction
old-fashioned ideals seemingly vanish
and myth and legend withdraw
to come upon the scene as time recurs
there is nothing not destroyed
by the smirk of the sun,
all are awakened
a new era dawns, affectionate
and comfortable
the light of the sun when it
glazes puts us to shame
sets aside the emotions
nay with promises many of resuscitation
●

OF DUSK

I am un aware, yes, unaware,
how tho' the lark sings at dawn,
running helter-skelter,
shouldering truck-like burdens,
tired, lying down,when the
entire worlds cometh to rest, thereone
hushed by the musk and held
as in a trance
donning the attire of lengths,
my gown dances at balls
captivating
does not the evening enter?
and filleth the ever-lasting?
the goblet of eternity?
ah! at nights reposing
when dusk invades,
quietly, I sleep
alas! I no longer know me!,
a nuance bothers me.

●

EMPHASIS ON SEASONS

Autumn dare approach
when all the cuckoos gonna sleep
it will be different
yes, different from what it had been,
these be times sought after
soothe like gelatin
myriad seasons, seemingly
reflections
O! father!, O! mother, I am blossoming
soon, it will be snowing in
all the alien countries
how happy I am to have you to care for!
my heart sings, let
there be no fare well
in your midst are my emotions
secure and bound
hard and fast
when the branches all of the trees
score the ground
we shall doze, in our minds
retain broad dreams, awaiting !,
Oooo h!, please God, let

the seasons fructify!
It`s spring and the cuckoos sing
landing on grass and plain
a well mowed lawn maintained
at home lets gather where there are
the primroses in plenty readily bloomed
looking up to the sky in adulation!
here, to find a shade, a temporary shelter blind
Nature redresses
some point there where my brother joins
my family under one umbrella below the sun
the spring rays not tormenting
for the flowers are only blooming,
their sashes, yet hidden from the light,
they have to remain smiling a long,
long time! and keep doing namaste,
we gaze, our soul cooled,
breathe easy, comforted
there is a delirium persisting tho'
when summer advances the heat is immense
Nature is reduced to be a hag
a bright future seemingly daunt
the incurable sickness to counter;
Nature's healing powers well questioned?
let spring come,
by which time we shall overcome!
emanate the prayer from our lips
●

PINING

Where there is a mango orchard and
a drumstick tree
that is my home
where I pine
●

PUMMELLO-LAND OF DESSERTS

Travelled into a mine of desserts
t'was laden with treacle pudding,
marmalade, tarts and pies of chocolate,
muffins, jam rolls and cake
pieces of the plain, plum
and cocoa variety,
baby pudding and cream,
milk pudding, shakes, fruit, pista,
orange, pineapple, mixed fruit,
whirlpools of broth, porridge, milk,
wafers, a dessert mine skiing which,
that takes you to revelry
and makes much of you oops!
delectable, wow! how delightful!.
Eat morsel after morsel and regain vitality.
Become replenished and totally so.

●

LONGEVITY AS PRONOUNCED

Today I am going to look ordinary
perchance it will make me beautiful, sometime else
but today is not a joke
I have to wholly involve, lest tomorrow haunt me,
Today I am going to win,
Today I realize I will come upon the truth and
I make obeisance,
Lord, please redeem me,
Today is meaningful, so, I must make it up,
Today I am going to smile
because it gives me the wings to fly,
Today, I'm gonna face
Today is made for me to be cheerful,
many days that come may not be,
Today I must save
Today I must be energetic
as tomorrow it may be impossible,
Today is to be lived and lived and lived
as it nurtures tomorrow,
a rightly promised hope.
●

A FATHOMLESS TRUTH

I do not know I am so wan
for I still have the gurgle of a baby 's laughter,
His rosy commands I still follow
tho' He be well gone now
eagerness I must clasp some more;
a day shall come, that I wait for
then I shall be merged,
fully merged in Him!
that is my aim,
that is my world,
that is the reality, I seek
when upon me, a door is not shut nor opened anymore
for I have completely merged along with the worlds
that is,
in His sublimity, in His Divine Self.

●

MY LOTUS FEET

Then one day, again He shall launch
in His majesty and prowess
and wherever He tread by His Holy Feet,
that land will be smiling and smiling
I can see the Lotus bloomed in profusion already
to pad up on to His tender soles
then also the one 's who waited be pleased, then,
cheer, laughter and merry- making return to the earth.

●

FEAR THAT GROOVES

Terror annulls my mantle
I dread being stomped by a stampede
mobbed in a crowd,
over shadowed and eclipsed by a darkness,
I fear being chunked like an apple,
marauded by bears whose hugs cramp my life
then, also superfluous light that exterminate
too much nausea by catering whiffs,
these are my imaginary fears....
I dread being done for in an assembly or
getting choked in an emotional battle
a shake- up when the goats bleat
and the thorough check-up
I encounter day after day after
day that maintains my health,
that I cannot learn much anymore
because my life shrinks
and penetrates within at intrusions
which are what I fear,
fear, fear and am in mortal dread of.

●

THE NULL AND THE VOID

I'd been howling like I'd viewed a horror matinee,
piteously, long I lay in convalescence,
wonderfully, today I gazed at a spectrum of light
that made me yonked to a frenzy of clouds
things changed as I bathed in the infinite blue,
I leashed at a May pole and twirled and twirled
forgetful of all the yanks of misery
time hath me in memory
I'm in a null tending to be a void
who acclaims ! Yes, God is great and powerful as well.

●

ALLEGIANCE

Is God going to come to my aid?
Is He going to respond to my prayer?
Is God going to be responsible for me?
Is God going to release me from the bondage of karma?
Is God going to give me ample freedom?
Is God going to give me His companionship?
Is God going to desert me in a forested island?
Is God, going to let me climb His ladder? up! ?.
Is God going to make me trail laboriously and make me
follow my pursuits without hindrance from outside?
Is God going to finally release me?
Is God doing this because
He does not will to let go off me?
Oh! God!, is my supplication to you,
going to be considered?
I owe you everything,
You are my All,
this is my allegiance.

●

JHULA

I drift, I am a gorgie, insecure,
I am a type, a personification of night,
light and day,
I scream, I belie,
I cry, I am fatigued,
I am immortal,
I can'st die,..
the precincts of my mortal
being resounds- a voice,
a feeble echo,
saying nay, nay,
I don't wanna perish
but I wish, wish to go high..
I wish to lie amidst hay,
hide roughly in the husks for
I am heady with wine
and intoxicated to extremes,
sadism within expresses sardonic likeness,
I wish I could be puffed up,
stretch wide and wide,
I am unheard..
I long to be released into the expansive sky,

with the freedom of a kite
to swing, swing, swing,
my life, being a jhula,
it takes at shot sorrow and joy,
pain and pleasure.
●

RELIEF

A dose of rain fall brings
the smile on an afflicted heart,
it raises the hope of feeble selves,
nothing is lost, nothing is lost,
I do not want to become meaner
coz I am feeling good,
gloom and grump have disappeared
there is only exultation over the self,
gratefullness,
and the greatness of being alive,
life appears good;
bad memories momentarily gone.

●

TO YOU, MY LORD

I hesitate presumptorily to ask
that, it be a delicate issue if,you fail to comply,
at times, your supply is quick, ah! that I ignore at risk,
I love it best when promises are readily kept,
my confidence never weakened
due to your many, signs of love,
Oh! God!, you shower boons,
you are kind!
I am subject to your mercy.

The Erratic is gone.
What 's up?
just see, the Sun has risen,
t'will wade over the mountains and
warm the ocean it 's rays will pierce the forest also
where Sita and Sri Rama have left their footprints,
isn't it gorgeous?!, the spectacle of the rising Sun!
it reacheth, my vicinity
it doth shine powerfully above the trees
and the terrace and the wild,
it's vibration is a marvel,
promotes excitement, compels living,
allows to rise above the erratic.
Wow!, behold!.

AM I UNDERRATED?

I won't always agree that I walk a blind path
nor that build a fence that
prosecutes tho' trespassers be many!,
I'm on a razor's edge, tyrrany,
memories ache
and I vouch forward in super-furgitive steps;
then time heals....
You are here.. bright, royal and new,
episodes slip by, -
I get at a truth,
that I be darned!
if I don't make it up with everyone,
a stark naked picture
that it pleases You, to see me smiling for
you can bear it all
and that 's why its ' been happening.
I don't want to be underrated.

●

FRITTER AND FLOURISH

When I die, I will be immortal,
living I am the same,
why then?,
I am sane
my apprehension and fears surely be torpedoed!?,
these botherations, I will transcend,
a new day will come by
when I will fritter and flourish.

●

RAIN-FALL THAT KEEPS PATTERING

The rain draped the velvety
earth with its monotonous
dialogue thunder erupted
the plains and lightning caught
up the sonata heaving on the throats
of delighted middle-men
whilst the folks put up a camp-fire
in dire the needs to meet
what was left for those whose peril
slightly reduced
was to finish the chores
there remained not much to be done
for Nature resumed its role
characteristic
playing an advanced lead
it poured and poured
simply to announce its pleasure
till all the men were persuaded
to yield their tools
O! wonder of nature pour on and on
we welcome thee

thy entrancing dance
it is good to pray, cried the simple-minded
good to surrender prophesied the religious monarchs
keep quiet a while commanded the elders to the robus-
tious young petrified but with hopes re-kindled
there is naught to fear
no catastrophe to alert
the temptations have ceased for
the skies above have descended
on the welcoming plains
the divine is welcome
God has come
Nature is alluring and really beckoning
we are in earnest
we are enchanted we are thrilled to
the core by the majesty of
Her prowess so let us huddle all the near
and dear one's
so let us chant un-perturbedly
the divine name,
glory to thee,
glory to thee.
●

THE GLOBE

To be on earth is to be
endeavouring
to be on earth is to put on a stint of bravado,
on earth worry ceases
because we are in the divine
Yen knowing that divine Will alone prevails
to be on earth is to follow
in the footsteps of the Lord-
His message being our command
to be on earth is to be unique as we are made,
to be on earth is so we love each other
to be on earth is to slowly
learn to ascend to where Bliss
preponderates.
●

HEARKEN TO THEE, MOTHER EVE

Here is she, Eve, who can't be fetched from
churches or gospel
nor does she thrive thro' debates concussing
she blushes at the very mention of her name
love being her paranoid
stupid when castigated
without ulterior motives
naive to reproach
starved when not propitiated
she is concerned about modesse
dump when mitigated
now she is strongly neglected, alas!
she is soothing to all and very pleasing
and can only be evoked thro' love,
her presence, alone, to embellish man.

●

FLUSTERED YET WITH HOPE

There were bubbles in the streams
when it rained catapult
and the wind gushed upon the clothes of man
now the disease has finally vanished
said the sunshine which promised to rise again
when God forgives man
health will come zooming back
it will be the planet's wealth
the boon awarded to the entire living species,
keeping to the rules and praying will do it for us.

●

TRANSCENDENTAL NOUMENA

When hours stretch long or
become fractions,
time lingers,
love harps in a forgetful consciousness
that has no botheration of day or night
or of relatives, far, near,
in that wakeful, positive note
bliss comes of it's own accord,
the bliss of sweetness of union with Love,
thy self and God,
that transcendental noumena,
called supra-efforrescence,
that is attractive,
nameless a condition attained by the
ones who avoid the crooked and are bent upon the
straight-forward routes.
naught else, worth possessing!

Timelessness is what I speak of or
the unveiling of a portraiture,
as it prevails a sudden gush of joy,
that is when the door is opened wide
permits breath-taking access to
a freedom that is limitless,
the breeze ruffles permeating joy,
when the curtain is drawn,
happiness, comes uncalled
when not intimidated,
it is surrender and prayer as well,
it is the awe when dark is gone,
yes, eternity is speechless pertaining,
the wealth of promises to
draw from future remedials,
is the wonder we hear of,
not me, but this,
is the Ultimate, Bhagawan, verily Himself.
●

EAVES-DROPPED SUDDENLY

We are making days out of hypnotic,
teasing, melodramatic contortions,
raked upon mankind several months back,
eaves-dropped suddenly, one time,
continuing it's troublesome havoc,
the sickness is yet unvanquished,
proceeding to renovate, whatever,
understandably remains at distance
 from pious minded persona,
flirting in the streets
drawing out comic situations-
maketh a vicious circle for those who fall
the one's who fall,
will they be remembered! ?
and what of solving the riddle?
that is to make a careful drama of life?!
there be sun-shine and glimmer
of the moon upon the earth here
and man wanna grow proud and immortal
nobody likes to die
nobody likes to go away
dis-heartened and chastened,

hearken! life
let man live!
its not as though God will neglect
but He will walk right into man's habiliment
and invite him to His own bourgeois Vista.
●

SELF-APPRAISAL

I am spiritually agile
responsive to goodness and care bestowed
only prone to the world 's diseases
that plunder and benumb
a frail structure that is what I am
floods of myopia darken my two eyes
and storm my psyche
invading my brain
making it lose reasonability
it caters to me
whets my appetite
the joy and longing for various
delectable pools and pools of water
that stretch yonder and yonder
I'd love to play in these waters absorbed
never retaliating or making a pun of what 's the world
because I fancy and appraise
that I got to belong here itself,
that I must do so
before it is too late or nigh impossible.
●

LET ME BE

Laughter, froth and liquor,
merry- making in excess makes me heady, weedy,
satiated I ought to cry,
Oh! Lord!
revive my senses
you, alone will return my kindness
my welp may pass unnoticed,
crap and nonsense kinda remarked
mostly I am calm
then tranquility enchants!,
I see you are in melancholy-
trap this vagrant tendency of my mind
I wish not that I be a vagabond
piteously, my passions are exhausted
I abhor the violence of the world
I am desire less, without agitations, yet
must I delve deep
for I am sorry
I cannot do much but love you
and gaze upon your form,
very much enrapt, please God,
let me be.

●

OF CO-OPERATION
AND THE ANANDA IT BESTOWS

Nondescript, incomprehensible, gillespie,
agaatha, indestructible,
knoweth not emptiness or void,
the pleasing is truth revealed step by step
not ever fluttering even upon
strong gushes of the wind,
immovable substrate
how so we gain its essence is how
we of the earth cognize the imperilous
taking breaths and breaks,
never doubting that it is hard
to tackle by one man or
a single- hearted effort never does achieve
mis-understanding never,
the truth is reprehensible,
bestowed on kind and gentle folks
that we have to join hands
in endeavour and stern
and blend and co- operate ;
if only we wish to be furbished.
Ah! that is joy.

●

SONATA TO MOST BELOVED BHAGAWAN SATHYA SAI BABA

I remember how I had once been a gal with hundred,
thousand dreams that did finally lead to thee
that I landed in thy holy abode
preliminarily the coveted
spot on the Buvaikunda called Puttaparthi
the encounter
which made me bigger and bigger
so fast to approach are you,
my Lotus Feet are hard to clutch
the inevitable that happened was your exit
my body trembles
encased in different habitation
I recall the spoilt years,
fond, dear memories
let the trains whistle
and the birds chirp
the mud clamp the foot- prints of holy men,
once more,
of those who tread the holy land Puttaparthi
let the goodness between us branch forth,
let my shivering cease.

●

TO YOU,
MY OWN SELF

Its only one life, mine, amongst countless others,
incomplete, with imperfections that I try to dodge,
yet full,bright and whole
like the whiteness of summer
does the light of my life skip
yes! I'm a gal with concealed excitement
and choked emotions
that lay bare the cold ice of winter
ah! I am exposed to the current
day after day I summon the energy
to dole out my life
play, enact, enrole
I beg pardon of you, visitor be kind to me
I care for your company
tho' solitude is my solace;
I cannot say further upon the truth
my happiness is life lived through
if you ask me ?!,
I am replete
finding joy within.

●

POSSESSED!

I staggered miles and miles
seemingly for an offense unpardoned
the evil returneth
with it's vigour of vendetta
to haunt persistently my
life times long
nay ! I hope too much
draw easy at sympathy
but then hardly harps remedy
for the force thus marshalled
wilt continue it's onslaught
unless dealt with deliberate storms of precaution
trailing my nervy edges
and the frail stuff of which my body is made.
ah! nowadays I 've come to compound a truth
tho' I can hardly bear it and am suffocated,
there be this hand which holds
wafting gently with care everywhere I go and fanning
I am secure thus in those arms
albeit, lacking understanding
because the power which thus enthuses
reacheth close upon my vicinity

and I am slowly cured of my insanity
thus am I loosened slowly from vast encumbrances
and feel uplifted highly and triumphantly
I, then dream of liberation.
●

OF DELICATE VARIETIES

I don't want to be like cabbage leaves
as of the past
but of lettuce or cauliflower
as you made me
that is savoured with relish
and good appetite
thus must I perceive more a value for my own person
for I am of delicate variety
true! my submission to thee is enrapturing!.

●

INHABITABLE EARTH

What of the distress and distemper?
ah!, the earth is upheld, as of yore
the living emerge from their hiding,
the sacred groves
into the land of similar facilities
affected from it's broken affluent past,
monastic temperaments evolved
acclimitazion invaded
a sudden recovery inimitable;
repeated wonders of God,
that earth may resound in clarion calls,
be inhabitable,
that mankind may thrive!.

●

MIGHT

I can see a future yawning
I needs must cater to it's whims
it's fancies are suitably met
what like is my sleep?,
I unwillingly enroll
leaving my burden to might
the force- full power
that is, God.

●

NOTCHED

I am awake
and going to play a game,
funnily, life has been made out to be
complicated an issue,
t'is hard to get to know the parlance
of the common man,
vexed and notched,
days ahead stare,
I don't get to understand the behavior
patterns anymore
what is that I am waiting for?,
alas!, I am tickled by stupendous
surprises,
I wanna badly go out
but, oh!, there is nowhere I'm eager
to tread.

●

AWE AND PITY

The likes of me shall bloom again
as lily is fond of the pond
is maintained thus
wavering petals too drop with time
that is how it shall be
life jumps at ease as a game with
snow balls
what lays bare is wisdom
which comes from life itself
wind captures a dahlia in terror
similarly shall life be swallowed
by storm of instigating torment of
insecurity;
- if you do not care,
let the likes of poor, weak selves loom large
so much as a moon hath light which
steadies the trembling....,
moveth a self over awed with pity

●

FROM THY VERY SELF

I don't know why it is on earth
deemed that you are put to tests and
trials,
tribulations that wrench your heart
which if you emerge victoriously from,
unscathed
your category is honoured, the zeal
for life made tempting,
when somehow you forget the
botherations,
life is made interesting, light and
attractive with changes.
It would appear finally a repertoire, as
to who is who and wherefore is that source
that we are seeking;
we are of the same origin, are we not?.

●

I AM A TRICKLE OF WATER

I am great but not that much I make
myself out to be
nor do I know what others imply
by the statement me
I rate me as fantastic
engrossed in love
preoccupied and miserly at
understanding another
the viewpoint regarding who I really
am!,
I understand I must really be raiment,
illusion likely to God Himself
I must be the shadow
cool as cucumber
and pale as the moon
I am the guarantee He vouch- safes
by,
I am, I think, a trickle of water
wanting to relinquish pride, -
my reality, it is hard to come by.

●

THE DIVINE EMBRACE

Oh! I do wish it would be over all too soon
I hurt me' self again and again
dabbed and lounged on the petals of lotus flowers
huddled as a heap
I would not like to budge
save a care- takers warning bell
there a person shouts
I can 'st hold on
I'm fast held in the divine embrace
loving the cuddle and cuddle of his disarming arms

●

PRECIOUS, PRECOCIOUS THE JEWEL CALLED LIFE

Life is one saga of loneliness, infatuation, brooding, constraint, heaving sorrow, mirth and merry-making, hardly any encounter, expensive, cheap exhibition, at times, difficult to be regular about, appeasement of the senses, lounge and loiter, roaming of the mind, wonder and wander, surrender and submission to authority, fun and jokes, musing, moods traversing, variable, sullen and joyous, augustness, tempo, cleansing, winding, calm and composed prefer to be, searching, stretching, longing, crying, bitter and sweet episodes, inviting, mixture of pleasure and contentment, weary, drowsy, low, lowly, becoming, powerful and

courageouseness, bravado, smiling,
full of obstacles, thorns to be
avoided, a lesson to be learnt, fitness, survival.....
●